This colourful book covers numbers 1 to 10.
Each number is illustrated with pictures
of familiar objects which children
will enjoy counting and naming.

Practice is given in matching, sorting and
counting through a variety of lively colour
pictures, making this book both fun and
invaluable for all young children
who are learning to count.

Available in Series 921

*†a for apple
*†let's count
*what is the time?
*shapes and colours

Also available in square format Series S808 *and*
†*as* Ladybird Teaching Friezes

First edition

Published by Ladybird Books Ltd Loughborough Leicestershire UK
Ladybird Books Inc Auburn Maine 04210 USA
© LADYBIRD BOOKS LTD MCMXCII
Printed in England (3)

let's count

illustrated by LYNN N GRUNDY

Ladybird Books

1

one

•

2

two

3

three

●●●

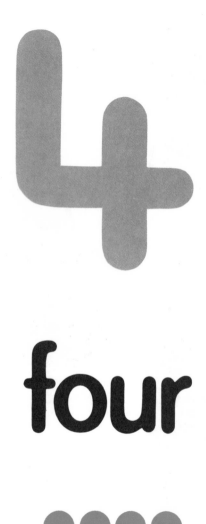

four

5

five

● ● ● ● ●

6

six

seven

8

eight

●●●●●●●●

9

nine

●●●●●●●●●

10

ten

●●●●●●●●●●

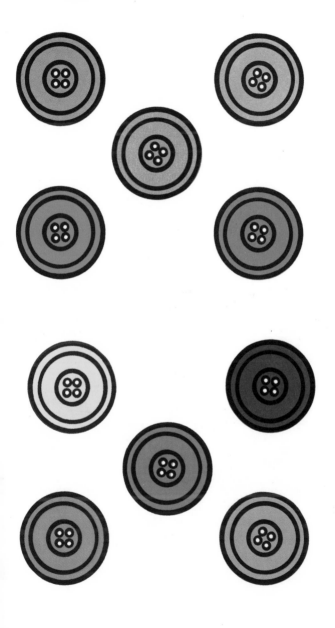

How many people in the bus?

How many are waiting for a ride?

How many people altogether?

How many...

bats?

toadstools?

spiders?

frogs?

snails?

How many monkeys are there?

Can each monkey have
a banana?

Which cars will be number 2,
number 5 and number 9?

Who is driving car number 7?